The Man Who Tricked a Ghost

BY LAURENCE YEP · PICTURES BY ISADORE SELTZER

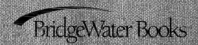

BridgeWater Books

To Jesse, who's never afraid of the difficult road.   *L.Y.*

To all those who love to get scared out of their wits.   *I.S.*

Once there was a man named Sung
who was very brave. Nothing scared him.
He would picnic in graveyards and nap in
haunted houses.

"We are all forms of the same thing," he
liked to say, "which makes us all cousins.
So why should I be afraid?"

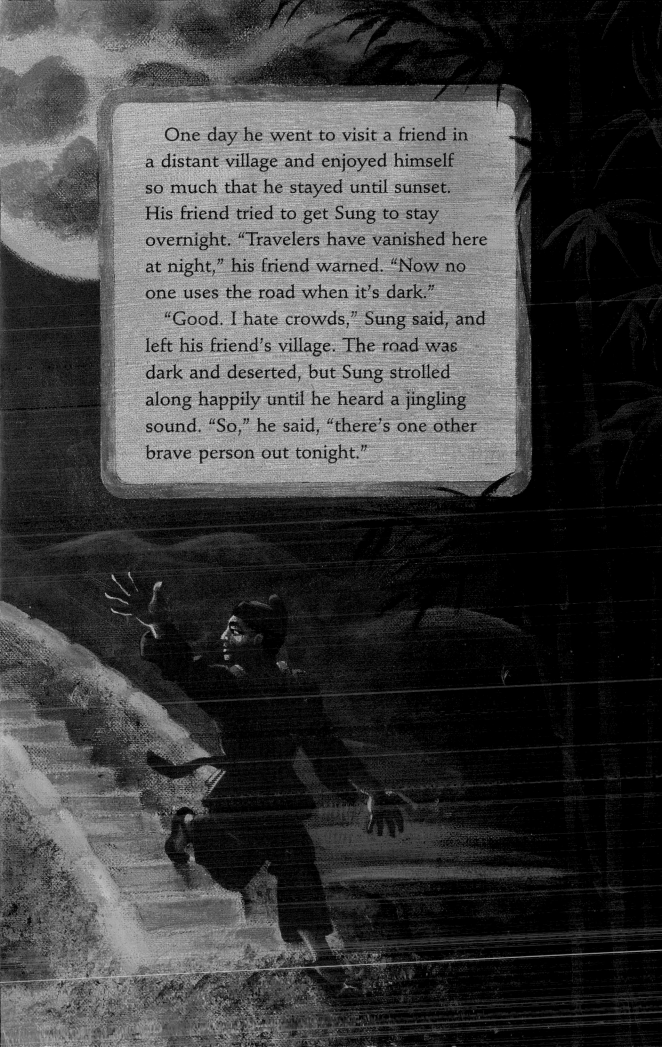

One day he went to visit a friend in
a distant village and enjoyed himself
so much that he stayed until sunset.
His friend tried to get Sung to stay
overnight. "Travelers have vanished here
at night," his friend warned. "Now no
one uses the road when it's dark."

"Good. I hate crowds," Sung said, and
left his friend's village. The road was
dark and deserted, but Sung strolled
along happily until he heard a jingling
sound. "So," he said, "there's one other
brave person out tonight."

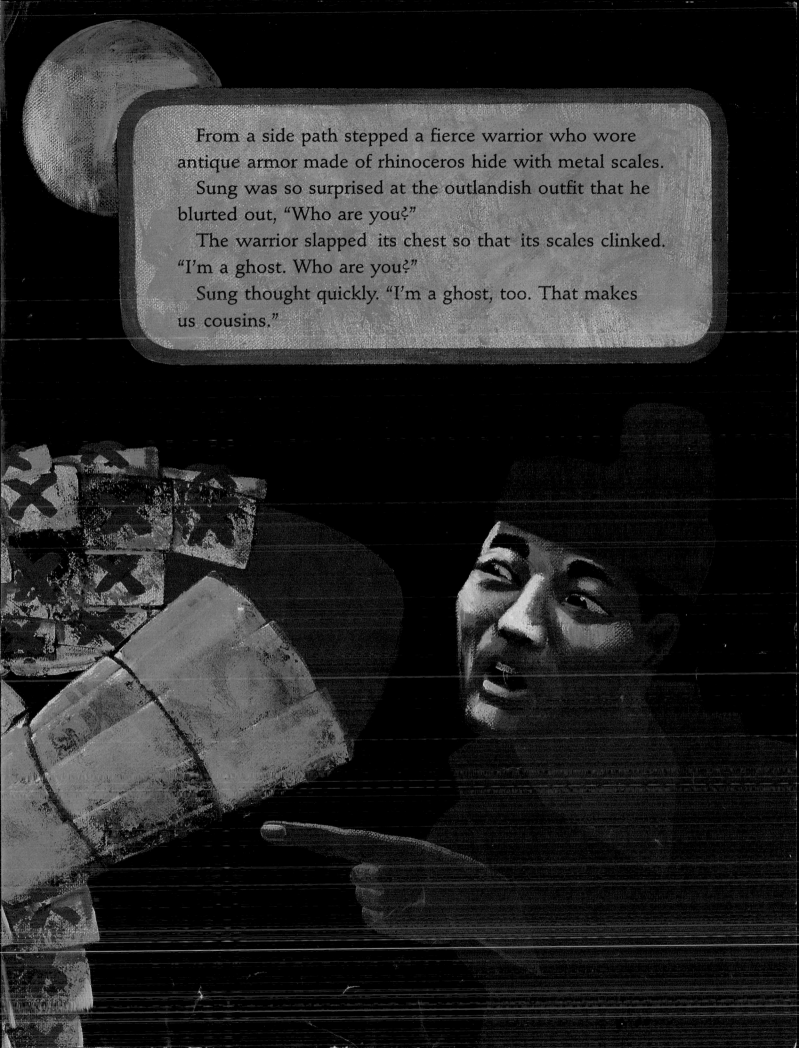

From a side path stepped a fierce warrior who wore antique armor made of rhinoceros hide with metal scales.

Sung was so surprised at the outlandish outfit that he blurted out, "Who are you?"

The warrior slapped its chest so that its scales clinked. "I'm a ghost. Who are you?"

Sung thought quickly. "I'm a ghost, too. That makes us cousins."

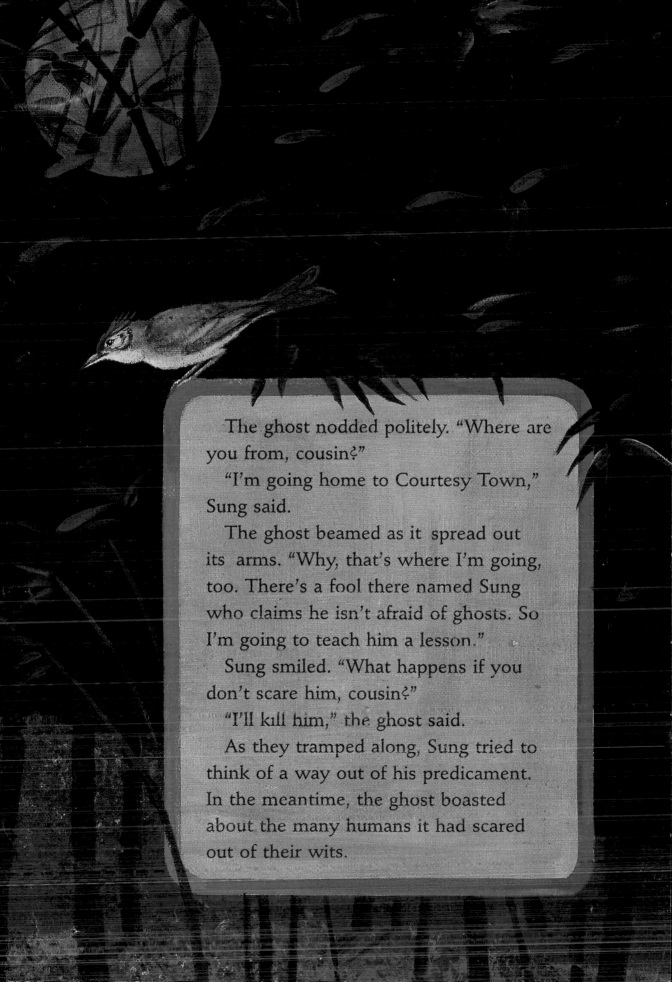

The ghost nodded politely. "Where are you from, cousin?"

"I'm going home to Courtesy Town," Sung said.

The ghost beamed as it spread out its arms. "Why, that's where I'm going, too. There's a fool there named Sung who claims he isn't afraid of ghosts. So I'm going to teach him a lesson."

Sung smiled. "What happens if you don't scare him, cousin?"

"I'll kill him," the ghost said.

As they tramped along, Sung tried to think of a way out of his predicament. In the meantime, the ghost boasted about the many humans it had scared out of their wits.

After a few miles, the ghost halted. "It's a long walk to Courtesy Town. Why don't we take turns carrying each other?"

Sung couldn't think of an excuse, so he agreed. "You can carry me first," he said.

When the ghost squatted down, Sung climbed on its back. The ghost grunted. "You're awfully heavy for a ghost."

Again, Sung thought quickly. "I'm new. I'll grow lighter when I get to be as old a ghost as you."

After another mile, the ghost announced it was Sung's turn and set him down on his feet. "Just how do you plan to scare Sung anyway?" he asked the ghost.

"Watch this!" The ghost's hair rose up in flaming spikes like twisted sword blades.

Sung, however, wasn't the least bit impressed. "I knew Sung quite well when I was alive. He'll just tell you to comb your hair."

"Wait. That's not all!" the ghost bragged. Its eyes started to glow a blood red and then it jerked off its head.

Sung merely yawned. "Since he can't afford candles, he might ask you to lend him your head as a lantern."

The gho
palm. "Thi
should jus

Sung sho
other hum
ghosting, I

"Done,"
shoulders,
ghost weig
under his b

They cha
switch, the
than the ot
of the ghos

Finally, as an irritated ghost slid onto his back, Sung said, "I've answered all your questions about Sung. Now it's your turn to answer my questions about being a ghost. What frightens us the most?"

"*Sh*. We never talk about that," the ghost warned. "Somebody might overhear."

Hiding his disappointment, Sung questioned his passenger about other ghostly secrets instead.

When they came to a stream, Sung set the ghost down at the edge of the water. "You first," he said.

Silently, the ghost drifted across the water to the other bank. Not a ripple disturbed the surface. Of course, when Sung tried to cross, he splashed loudly.

The ghost stared at him as he climbed out of the stream. "You're awfully noisy for a ghost."

As Sung climbed dripping onto the riverbank, he scolded the ghost. "Didn't your parents teach you any manners? Don't make fun of me just because I'm not as expert a ghost as you."

The ghost was so ashamed that he tried to apologize, but Sung shook his head. "If you really wanted to make up for your rudeness, you'd tell me what to watch out for."

Feeling guilty, the ghost leaned close to Sung's ear to whisper, "Watch out for human spit."

"Why?" Sung whispered back.

The ghost shuddered. "Because once we are spat upon we cannot change our shape."

The ghost still had not found a scary enough form when they reached Courtesy Town the next morning. However, Sung urged the ghost to come with him so it could see its enemy's home.

Disguising himself as a farmer, the ghost walked side by side with Sung. Because it was market day, there was a large crowd of people on the road. There were farmers with baskets of vegetables, fishermen with trout fresh from the river, and shepherds with whole flocks of sheep.

When they were near the gates, Sung pounced upon the ghost and easily lifted it over his shoulder. "Let me go!" the ghost shrieked.

"I'm going to take you to the temple and have the priest destroy you," Sung said, and ran through the gates and into the center of town. "Make way, everyone! I've caught a ghost!"

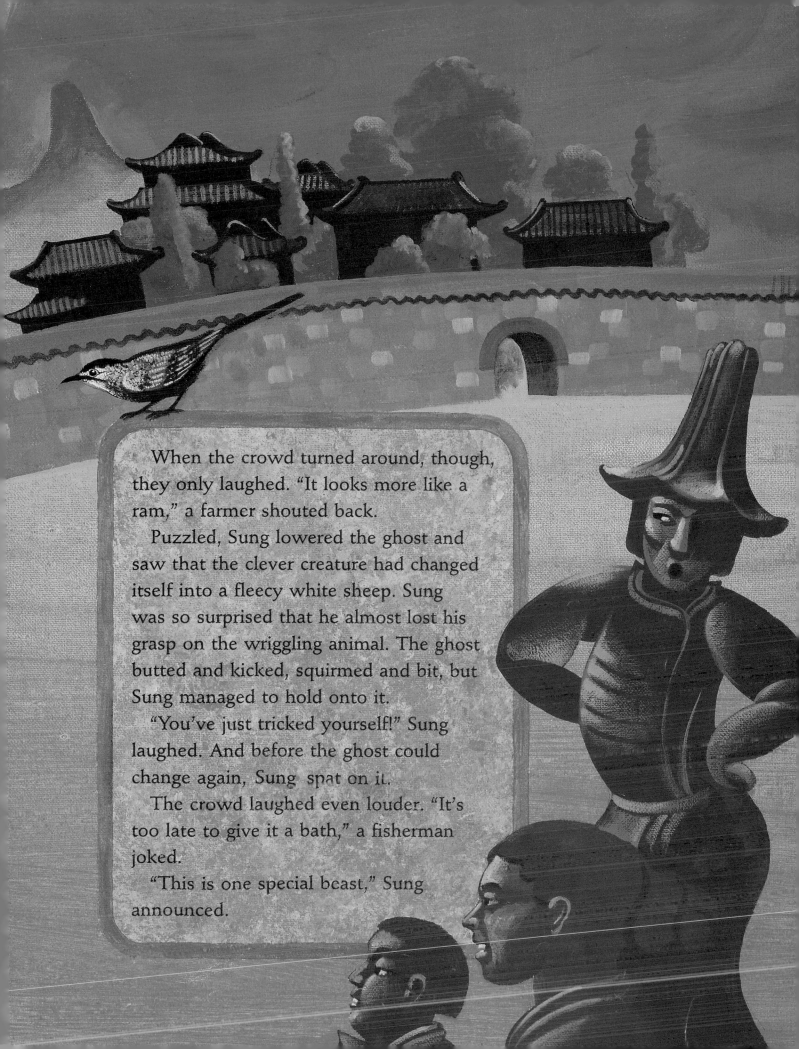

When the crowd turned around, though, they only laughed. "It looks more like a ram," a farmer shouted back.

Puzzled, Sung lowered the ghost and saw that the clever creature had changed itself into a fleecy white sheep. Sung was so surprised that he almost lost his grasp on the wriggling animal. The ghost butted and kicked, squirmed and bit, but Sung managed to hold onto it.

"You've just tricked yourself!" Sung laughed. And before the ghost could change again, Sung spat on it.

The crowd laughed even louder. "It's too late to give it a bath," a fisherman joked.

"This is one special beast," Sung announced.

The shepherds had to agree. None of them had ever seen a sheep with fleece as fine as the ghost's. They fought one another to buy it, until Sung finally sold the ghost for 1,500 copper coins.

Jingling the many strings of cash in his hands, he started off for home. If he was new at being a ghost, he was even newer at being rich.

But he liked it.

The original story of the man who tricked a ghost was first published in the third century A.D., making it one of the first ghost stories to appear in print in China. An emperor himself was said to have written it down.